Joseph Alden

The Light-Hearted Girl

A Tale for Children

Joseph Alden

The Light-Hearted Girl
A Tale for Children

ISBN/EAN: 9783744666299

Printed in Europe, USA, Canada, Australia, Japan

Cover: Foto ©Andreas Hilbeck / pixelio.de

More available books at **www.hansebooks.com**

THE

LIGHT-HEARTED GIRL;

A

TALE FOR CHILDREN.

BY

JOSEPH ALDEN, D. D.,

AUTHOR OF THE "GREAT SECRET DISCOVERED"

———◆———

BOSTON:

J. E. TILTON AND COMPANY,

161 WASHINGTON STREET.

1863.

PREFACE.

"The Light-Hearted Girl" is intended to be the first volume of a series similar in character and design. The object of the writer will be perceived by the parent who reads the book; and every parent should previously read the book which he places in the hands of his children. Perhaps he will find, in the incidents and examples furnished by this volume, and those which may follow it, helps in the cultivation of right habits of thought and feeling on the part of those for whose education he is in so high a degree responsible.

"The Cardinal Flower," the second of the series, will be published in a few weeks.

CONTENTS.

LIGHT-HEARTED GIRL.

CHAPTER I.

THE PLAYHOUSE AND FURNITURE—THE DOLL.

"O mamma, do come and see my house! It is so perfectly beautiful, I don't believe any body ever had such a nice house, and so many pretty things in it. Please, mother, come and see it."

These words were spoken by a bright-eyed, curly-haired girl, about eight years of age.

The mother laid aside her sewing and followed her little daughter. Her house was under an apple-tree which stood near the door. Its limbs were loaded with fruit, which caused their extremities to touch the ground. There was an open space through which you might enter, and then you were shaded from the sun, and concealed from view by the foliage. It was a charming place for a playhouse; only it would not shed rain; but children should be in the house when it rains.

Jane had laid some pieces of board on the grass for a floor; and on some blocks, for tables, she had set out her furniture. This consisted of several pieces of broken crockery, three or four spools on which cotton had been wound, a couple of paper boxes which had contained hooks and eyes, a wooden knife and fork which a good-natured boy had made for her, and several wooden spoons which she had made for herself: perhaps you would not have known that they were meant for spoons unless she had told you.

But there was one thing more, which she thought was more valuable than all the other things she had. It was her doll.

I will tell you how she came by it. One day her mother sent her to the store to get some needles. Mr. Jones was just opening a crate of earthen flower-pots; and among them there was an earthen man, about as long as your hand. I don't know how it came in among the flower-pots. Mr. Jones gave it to Jane. She was delighted with it, for she saw that she could dress it, and make a doll of it. She had never had a doll except one that was made of rags. But now she could have a doll with a face, and nose, and mouth.

She dressed it very neatly, and thought it would have been perfectly beautiful, if it had only been white. But she was well satisfied with it as it was, and thought a great deal of it, as appears from the expression recorded above, " I don't believe any body ever had so nice a house, and so many pretty things in it."

Perhaps the reader may have a great many costly playthings, and may be disposed to say that Jane was foolish in thinking so much of her broken crockery and boxes. But I think it quite likely that she derived more pleasure from her playthings than you do from yours.

The reason was, she was easily contented. She enjoyed what God had seen fit to give her. She was not longing for what belonged to others. ˙

Jane's mother went with her, and stooped down, and got into her house. She tried to sympathize with her daughter in her happiness, but there was a sadness in her smile which was not unobserved by Jane, and which damped her spirits a little ; for she might be said to live in the life of her mother. Mrs. L. was a widow, and was poor. She earned her daily bread by the labor of her hands. She was often obliged to wake and toil while others slept.

In her younger days she was far removed from want. When she was a child, she had playthings of every description — dolls dressed in silks — little china tea-sets — and sofas, and chairs, and many such things.

As she compared Jane's playthings with those which she used to have, the contrast made her sad for a moment ; but when she saw that Jane was quite as happy as she used to be, her sadness gave place to gratitude. She thanked God that such simple things could give so much happiness to her darling child.

She sat down and played company with Jane, though she had to sit up till midnight to make up for lost time.

CHAPTER II.

JANE'S CHEERFULNESS — THE NEW FROCK — A NOBLEMAN.

One day Jane came in from her playhouse, and said, "Mother, I feel just like the little wren, who has his nest in the beam, in the woodhouse."

"How is that, my dear?"

"Why, I feel as if I wanted to *chipper, chipper, chipper,* all the time."

"Well, you may chipper as much as you please. You know I am always glad to see you happy."

"But, mother, I sometimes feel as though I ought not to enjoy myself so much, while you have to work so hard. I wish I could help you."

"You make me happy by being happy; and you do help me a great deal."

This was true; for, young as Jane was,

she washed the dishes, and swept the room, and did a great deal of the house work.

One day, as Jane came home from one of the neighbors, her mother said to her, "I'm sorry to tell you, darling, but I must, — that I can't get you the new frock we talked about. Mrs. H. has concluded to make the rest of Mr. H.'s shirts herself, and I can't pay for the calico."

She tried to smile when she said this, but she could not. . Indeed, she looked as though her heart ached very badly.

Little Jane threw her arms around her neck, and kissed her, and said, "No matter, mother; I can do without it."

Now, many little girls would have felt sorely disappointed, and would have made some complaints, and thus increased the care and sorrow of the mother.

Who could help loving such a girl? and yet there are persons in the world who will say and do things adapted to make such a girl very unhappy.

Not long after the event above noticed, Jane happened to be where there were a good many girls and boys collected together.

2

She had on a frock that was very clean, but it was a good deal patched.

"I wouldn't wear a frock with so many patches," said a dark-complexioned girl, with very dirty teeth, and a fine calico dress soiled with several grease-spots. "I wouldn't wear a frock with so many patches."

"You would, if your mother was not able to get you another one," said Jane, — not angrily, but with a tone of sadness that touched the heart of James Ferry, who overheard the insulting remark.

"Well, my mother isn't too poor, nor my father, neither. I've got ever so many frocks besides this."

"You ought to be thankful for them, then," said James, sternly, "and not try to hurt the feelings of a poor girl, who is as good as you are, and better too."

"O dear!" said the little aristocrat: but the steady gaze of James's indignant eye made her quail and keep silence.

James went home, and told his father what had occurred in relation to Jane, and what he had said.

James's father was a nobleman. " What!" methinks I hear a reader say, "a nobleman! Dukes and lords are noblemen. Are there any noblemen in this country?"

Yes, there are some true noblemen in this country: men who think, feel, and act, in a noble manner. James's father was one of these. He praised his son for his sympathy with the poor widow's daughter; and when James asked him if he could afford to give Jane a frock, he told him to go to the store and get one from any piece he chose. There was something in his eye that looked very much like a tear, but a proud smile was upon his lips.

The next day a small bundle was left at Mrs. L.'s door, with Jane's name upon it. She wondered who sent it. " I wish I knew whom to thank for it: I think I never saw so pretty a piece of calico in my life." After a moment's silence, she added, "Why, mother! I wonder I did not think. The good Lord has made somebody send it, and I must thank him for it!" And she went into her bedroom, and kneeled down, and returned thanks to God.

CHAPTER III.

THE RUDE BOYS—THE FATE OF THE DOLL.

One day, when Jane and her mother were away from home, two rude boys came along, and spied Jane's playhouse. They went in, and looked with contempt on her little treasures.

" What a playhouse ! " said one.

" Good enough for poor folks," said the other.

" See, what a doll !—a mulatto, I declare ! I'll make her show her teeth."

And he took a stone and struck the doll's mouth, in order to break off the glazing ; but the blow broke off its head.

" There, you've done it now, Jim ! "

" No matter ! She will never find out who did it. If she does, she can't hurt us."

" She will tell her mother."

" No matter for that. She is only a widow ; what can she do ? " and he threw away the head, and put the doll where he found it.

Now, if those boys had known how much poor little Jane thought of her doll, and how sorry she would feel to find it broken, would they have acted as they did? I am afraid they were hardened, unfeeling boys; otherwise they would not have spoken as they did of the widow.

When Jane found out that the head of her doll was missing, she felt very badly, as you may suppose. She wept by herself for a time, and then went to her mother. " Mother, I must tell you, though you can't help it. Somebody has broken off the head of my doll."

" I wonder who could do such a thing!" scarce able to refrain from tears in view of her daughter's distress.

" I should not think any body could be so hard-hearted," said Jane.

Does any one say, " What a fuss to make about an old earthen doll!" Remember, it was a great matter to her feelings; and that is the way in which you ought to regard things. Nothing is to be regarded as

2 *

trifling which deeply affects the feelings of a fellow-creature.

"My dear," said Mrs. L., "comfort yourself with the thought, that God would not have suffered it to take place, if he had not seen that it was for the best. It has happened by the permission of the same Providence which caused the dress, which gave you so much joy, to be sent to you."

"I remember, mother, that I read in the Bible this morning —" and she went and turned to the chapter and read, "Shall we receive good at the hand of the Lord, and shall we not receive evil?"

She dried her tears. For some time, whenever she thought of her doll, she felt unhappy for a moment; but she comforted herself in the way pointed out by her mother.

CHAPTER IV.

THE BLUE SKY — THE CLOVER-FIELD — THE BREAKFAST.

It was a beautiful summer morning. The sun was not yet risen. There was not a cloud to obscure the bright azure of the sky.

Jane and her mother were up, and at their work; for the industrious poor rise early. Sometimes, when she rose very early, Jane's mother would try to get up so softly as not to awaken her daughter; but she rarely succeeded. She used to tell Jane that it was as easy to cheat a pussy-cat asleep as to cheat her — a comparison which pleased Jane very much.

Jane always rose with her mother, and always rose in good humor. I have seen children whom it was not safe to speak to before breakfast, they were so snappish. But Jane could always smile as soon as she could get her little eyes open. Don't you suppose she was happier, and made others happier, than if she had a sour lip and a don't-speak-to-me look?

Jane sat by the door, which was thrown open, that the fresh air, and the fragrance from a neighboring clover field which was in its glory, might come in. She was winding some silk for her mother; or rather was holding the skein on her fingers while her mother wound it. She kept looking up to the sky very earnestly, but not so as to fail to hold the silk properly.

"What do you see that interests you so much?" said her mother.

"The sky, mother," replied Jane.

"Is there any thing unusual in its appearance?"

"No, ma'am. I was only thinking how beautiful it is — so blue, and even, and arching. It makes one feel bright to look at it. Mother, did you ever think how it would look if it were of some other color?"

"I don't know as I ever did."

"I was thinking, a little while ago, that it might have been brown, or black. How

awful it would have looked then! How
kind it was in the good Lord to make it
blue; it is *so* beautiful."

"The Lord does all things well."

"I know it, mother, and I wonder, seeing
he does all things so well, that folks can't
do better."

Her mother was not pleased to hear this
remark; it looked as though Jane was
thinking of other people's faults instead of
her own. She did not reprove her, how-
ever, but simply asked, "Whom do you
mean?"

"All the people in the world. I wonder
they are not better and happier. It is not
the Lord's fault."

"You are one of the people in the
world."

"I know it: that was what I was thinking of. I wondered, when I saw the sky
so bright, and the clover so sweet, that I
didn't love God more — that I ever neglect-
ed to try to please him."

"You do right, my dear, to let these
things remind you of your duty; and I
hope you will cherish the habit: but do not

forget your dependence on the grace of God."

"I'll try not to, mother; but is not every thing made as good and pretty as it can be?"

"I don't know: let us see," said her mother, willing to let her daughter exercise her thoughts: "what is the first thing you can name as showing the proof of your doctrine?"

Jane thought for a moment, and then said, "There is the clover — how could it have been made prettier? There is the green leaf, and the red blossom, and the sweet smell."

"Wouldn't it have been better if the blossom had been blue?"

"A blue clover-blossom! Who ever heard of such a thing?"

"You were admiring the blue color of the sky just now; you seemed to think it the best color ——"

"Yes, mother, for the sky, but not for clover-blossoms."

"Well, wouldn't the leaves have looked better if they were of a bright red?"

" O, no, mother. Red is very beautiful ; but then there would be too much of it. I should get tired of it, and it would make the eyes ache. Green never does, you know."

" Well, then, suppose the blossoms had the fragrance of the rose ; would not that be an improvement ? "

Jane could not answer this question as readily as she did the former ones. She loved the perfume of the rose very much, and she rather thought that it would be a fine thing to have every clover-blossom give forth this perfume, especially as roses were rather scarce about her mother's dwelling. But pretty soon she made the following reply : —.

" If every clover-blossom had the scent of the rose, it might be too strong to be pleasant. The scent of the lilach is very sweet ; but where there are a great many bushes, it is too strong."

" What else is there you can think of which is made as pretty and well as it can be ? "

" Well, there are the birds. How could

they be more beautiful than some of them are? and how could they be made to build prettier nests, or sing better?"

Mrs. L. smiled at Jane's reasoning, but thought it was quite as good as a great deal that passes for logic in the world; and she made no reply.

"Mother, *hasn't* the Lord made every thing as good and pretty as can be?"

"There are deserts in the world. God could have made them fruitful and smiling, could he not?"

Jane saw that she had framed her theory on too small a number of facts — a thing that older philosophers very often do. She made no reply to her mother's question.

"My dear, God has made every thing as wisely as it could be made, and that is all that we are at liberty to say. That is enough for us to know."

Jane looked a little disappointed. She looked as though she wished her doctrine were true.

"Why are you so anxious to have your doctrine true?"

"Because I thought, if it was so, it would

be a good reason why every body should be contented. If God has done every thing as well as he could, then every body ought to be satisfied with every thing. When I know you have done for me all you can do, I'm contented."

"Suppose you want something which I can do for you, but I don't think it is best for you. Can't you be contented then?"

"O, yes, mother."

"Why?"

"Because I know that you know, better than I do, what is best for me."

"That, my child, is the true ground of contentment and submission to God. He knows what is best for us, and will do it. Always remember this when you are tempted to repine."

The teakettle had now boiled, and they prepared their breakfast. This did not take long. Do you wish to know what they had for breakfast? Well, there was some tea, for Mrs. L., but no sugar. Jane always drank cold water. They had, also, some rye bread, and some molasses. That was all.

Many children would have cried for

something better.   But Jane folded her
little hands, and closed her eyes while her
mother asked a blessing, and ate her bread
and molasses with a thankful heart.

"When   I   get   those   handkerchiefs
hemmed, if Mrs. Carson pays me, we can
get a pound of butter."

"O, that will be nice, mother."

"Poor little thing!" thought her mother;
"she doesn't know what other children
have; she often thinks herself well off
with what beggars would not take!" But
such thoughts as these rarely entered Mrs.
L.'s mind, and were never cherished.   In
a moment, reflection had brought her to
feel thankful that her child could be happy
with what beggars would refuse.   She felt
that it was better than wealth.

CHAPTER V.

THE DISAPPOINTMENT—BUTTER AND HONEY

In the afternoon, the handkerchiefs were hemmed, and Jane carried them home. She took a little pail, that she might go to the store, and get some butter, if Mrs. Carson paid her.

Mrs. Carson was reading when Jane brought her the handkerchiefs. She examined and laid them down.

" Mother told me to ask you if they were done to please you," said Jane.

" They are done well enough," said Mrs. C. ; and she went on with her reading.

Jane stood waiting, not knowing what to do. Her mother had told her not to ask for the money, yet she was very unwilling to return without it.

" What are you waiting for ? " said Mrs. C.

" I wanted to get some butter," said Jane, timidly.

"I don't keep butter to sell. O, you want the money!" and she felt in her pock-et, and Jane's face lighted up; but it fell again when Mrs. C. added, "Come to-morrow; I haven't any change."

Jane kept from crying till she got out doors, but she could refrain no longer. She thought so much of having some nice bread and butter, and she had not had any for so long! She was going towards home look-ing very sad, when Mr. Ferry met her, and asked her what was the matter, and she very innocently told him the whole story, but not in a manner complaining of Mrs. C.

"Why didn't she send to the store for it then? But so it is: come to-morrow — and suffer in the mean time for what is wrongfully withheld!" Mr. Ferry uttered these words in an indignant tone of voice, which frightened Jane; she didn't know what he meant, and thought he was scold-ing her. But she was relieved from her fear by his saying to her, in a very kind voice, "Come with me, little girl; I'll get you some butter."

She went with him to his house, which

was not far distant. He took her pail, and caused it to be filled with butter, and re· turned it to her, saying, " Tell your mother I shall want some shirts made soon, and that the butter can go towards paying for them ; and tell her not to feel hurt at the liberty I have taken."

Jane thanked him from the fulness of her heart, and ran almost all the way home. As she entered the door, her mother, seeing her bright face, said, " So she paid you ? "

" No, ma'am, she told me to come to-morrow." Here the countenance of the widow fell. " But," continued Jane, " I've got ever so much butter."

" How did you get it ? "

" When I came away from Mrs. Carson's, I was crying, — I couldn't help it, I was so disappointed, — and Mr. Ferry met me, and asked what I was crying for, and so I told him, and he took me home with him, and filled the pail full of the nicest butter, — only see it, — and told me to tell you that he should want some shirts made soon, and that the butter might go towards paying for them ; and he told me to tell you not to feel

3 *

hurt at what he had done. I don't know
what he meant by saying so."

Jane had not been home long, before a
great, awkward, but honest-looking boy,
came in with a large white bowl carefully
covered with a napkin. "Mr. Ferry," said
he, "has been taking up bees, and sends
you some."

"Some bees?" said Jane, somewhat as-
tonished.

"Some what bees make," said the boy,
laughing; and he placed the bowl on the
table, and, taking off the napkin, discovered
several pounds of the whitest honey. "I'll
stop for the bowl when I come back."

"O mother, how nice! how sweet! how
good! what an excellent tea we shall have!
What a good man Mr. Ferry is!"

"And how good is the Lord, in whose
hand are the hearts of all men!"

CHAPTER VI.

THE VISIT—THE ROBIN'S NEST.

One afternoon, Jane went to visit Susan Green, a little girl who lived about half a mile distant from Mrs. L.'s. Susan seemed very glad to see her, and they played very pleasantly for an hour or so, when Margaret and Angeline Thorne came to see Susan also. They lived in a large white house, and their father was called a rich man. They were dressed quite gaudily, and in what their dress-maker was pleased to call the fashion. They did not speak to Jane, but stared at her very much as they had seen their mother stare at the "common sort of people," when they came too near her.

They had not been there long before they took Susan aside, and had a time of whispering with her. Jane thought their manners had not been well attended to, and she

turned and looked at the heartless girls, who were laughing and playing, and wondered that they could be so happy in sight of one they had treated so unkindly.

As she was walking along beside the fence, now and then wiping a tear from the corner of her eye with her apron, she saw something which looked like a little fan projecting above the middle rail in the fence, where the two lengths of rails joined together.

She went up to it, and what do you think it was? It was a robin sitting on a nest. Jane stood close to him, but he turned up his eye, and looked at her, and seemed to know that she would not hurt him.

She longed to put out her hand and smooth his brown coat, but she was so afraid of frightening him that she held her breath; and when she had looked at every feather on him, and seen him wink ever so many times, she moved slowly away till she was out of his sight, when she started and ran, and never stopped till she got home. "Mother! mother! I've found a robin's nest; and the old robin is so tame!

and it is so low down that I can look right into it. I was so close to him that I could see his little throat move when he breathed; and he never flew off. What do you think is in the nest?"

"I can't say," smiling at her daughter's enthusiasm and happiness.

"They must be either eggs or little young ones."

"Yes."

"Well, I hope they are eggs."

"Why?"

"Because it will be longer before they leave the nest, and I can watch them every day, and see when they hatch out, and see them grow, and have a nice time with them: and can't I feed them, mother?"

"I suppose you can; but I doubt whether the old birds will wish you to. They can take care of them themselves."

"But, mother, it must be such hard work for the poor little robins to go and look all over for one little worm, and carry it to the nest, and then go for more. Why wouldn't it be better for me to put a handful of crumbs right down by the nest, so that they could feed the young ones when they are hungry, and stay by them all the time?"

"My dear, the old birds know best what is good for their young, and will be most obliged to you if you will only let them alone."

"Do you suppose they take pleasure in working for their young?"

"I presume so: but why have you come home so soon?"

"O mother, I'm sorry you asked me."

"I hope my daughter has done nothing which she is unwilling to tell me."

"O, no; I've done nothing — only I had forgotten all about it since I found the robin's nest, and I don't wish to remember it."

"Tell mother what it was, dear."

"We were playing, Susan and I, and Susan was glad enough to have me there till Margaret and Angeline Thorne came, and then she told me to go home, for she didn't want me any longer now that she had other company; and the other girls laughed at me because I cried. So I came away, and when I saw the robin's wee bit tail peeping up, I forgot all about it, and I shouldn't have thought of it now, if you had not asked me why I came home. I don't think it was doing as she would like to be done by. But, mother, let us talk about the robin. Do you know, mother, what I think about the nest?"

"How should I know your thoughts?"

"I did not know but that my thought was wrong, and it always seems to me, that you know my thoughts when I do wrong."

"Let me hear your thought."

"Well, I think the good Lord told the robin to build his nest there, and to sit in it so that I could see him, in order to comfort me. Is it wrong to think so?"

"You have a right to view the robin's nest in that light. The nest was there in the providence of God for your comfort. I do not suppose that your comfort was the sole reason of its being there. But God caused it to be there, and he caused it to work for your good, and you owe him the same thanks that you would owe him, if the case were in all respects just as you have supposed."

CHAPTER VII.

SOMETHING MORE ABOUT THE VISIT — FORGIVENESS.

Susan did not enjoy the society of her new visitors as much as she did Jane's. She was soon sorry they had come. They found fault with every thing, and spoke so slightingly of Susan's things, that at length she became angry, and the result was a severe quarrel; and if Susan's mother had not interfered, perhaps there would have been some fighting and scratching. Susan's mother, who was not a very polished woman, said they acted like a parcel of dogs and cats. There was certainly some truth in the comparison.

Margaret and Angeline went home long before evening, declaring they would never speak to Susan again — a promise which they kept till the next time they saw her.

After they were gone, Susan had time to

4

reflect on her conduct towards Jane, and to contrast Jane's conduct with that of her other visitors. She felt sorry that she had treated her so badly ; but her sorrow was not because her conduct had been heartless and wrong, but because she had lost Jane's company, and had no one to play with her. She felt no real repentance.

She was cross, and discontented, and unhappy ; while Jane was cheerful and happy. When she left Susan, she did not leave with reproaches ; there was a load on her mind, but the robin's nest took it off; and for the remainder of the day she was very happy.

Does any one say, " She could not have felt very bad if so trifling a thing as a robin's nest could comfort her "? Reader, there are no trifling things in God's works. God has great designs connected with what some call trifling things. With this robin's nest were connected the happiness and improvement of an immortal soul.

At night, just before they were about to offer their evening prayer, Mrs. L. asked Jane, " What does the Saviour say about forg'veness ? "

" Where, mother ? "

" In the fifth chapter of Matthew and the fourteenth verse. Turn to the passage, and read it."

Jane took the Bible, and read, " For if ye forgive men their trespasses, your heavenly Father will also forgive you ; but, if ye forgive not men their trespasses, neither will your Father forgive your trespasses."

" Well, my daughter, we are about to ask God to forgive our sins ; is there any thing which you have not forgiven ? "

Jane was silent for a moment, and then answered, " I don't know, ma'am."

" Can you forgive Susan ? "

" I can, if she is sorry for what she has done."

" But suppose she is not ? "

" Ought I to forgive her, then ? "

" Certainly."

" I thought the Bible meant that they should ask forgiveness. I remember Christ says, ' If he turn and say, I repent, thou shalt forgive him.' If Susan is not sorry, she don't wish me to forgive her ; why should I ? "

" Because Christ wishes you to forgive her; you must forgive her for Christ's sake."

" I'm sure I will forgive her if Christ wishes me to ; but I can't feel towards her just as I should if she were to ask my forgiveness."

" It is not possible, nor is it necessary, for you to have the same feelings you would have in that case. Christ wishes you to feel no malice towards her, no desire to injure her, but a desire to see her good and happy."

" O, I can feel all that ; and after all, it was a small matter, since the robin's nest put it all out of my head. May I go and see the nest early in the morning ? "

Her mother gave her consent. They then kneeled and offered up their thanksgiving and prayer, and retired to their lodging-room. It was a plain room ; there was no carpet on the floor, and no furniture but a bed, a rude table, and two chairs. But the angels of God thought it was a privileged place, and did not disdain to remain there and watch the repose of the humble sleepers.

CHAPTER VIII.

JANE IN AN UNAMIABLE MOOD — SUSAN — ANOTHER VISIT TO THE NEST.

THE next morning, Jane awoke before the dawn; but she did not stir for fear of awaking her mother. Her mother had been very hard at work the day before. "She must be very tired," thought Jane, "and must sleep as long as she can."

I hope the reader will be equally considerate of the comfort of his mother and friends.

When Mrs. L. awoke and began to rise, Jane jumped out of bed like a grasshopper, and flew round the room to get her clothes.

"I'll be dressed first, mother!" and she hurried in a way a little unpleasant to her mother, who did not feel very well, and she reproved her, perhaps, not quite as gently as she usually did.

Jane looked a little put out, and began

4 *

to put on her clothes very slowly. In some children you would not have minded it at all, but you would have been sorry to see it in Jane. A small spot on a white dress shows very plainly.

Mrs. L. noticed Jane's ill humor, and said, "Are you angry with your poor old mother?"

Jane's heart gave way at this appeal.

"O, no, mother; forgive me!" and she threw her arms around her neck, and they mingled their tears together.

After breakfast, Jane asked her mother to go with her and see the robin's nest; but she answered, "I have too much to do: the poor have no time for morning walks."

This was spoken in a complaining tone, which made Jane feel unhappy. She loved to hear her mother speak, as she usually did, in a different tone, and say of hardships, "It is no matter, it is all right." Then she felt as if she could put up with almost any thing.

Mrs. L. very seldom spoke in this complaining manner. Do you ask why she ever did? I reply, she was not perfect, though she was a very pious woman.

Jane went alone to the nest. On the way she saw a little girl coming along the road, and pretty soon she saw it was Susan. "She is coming to make up," said Jane to herself, and she prepared to give her an encouraging look.

But when Susan saw Jane, she turned and ran the other way. "The wicked flee," thought Jane, "when no man pursueth." She could not help laughing to see her look back to see if she was followed. "On the whole," thought Jane, "it is as well she ran away. She would have gone with me to the nest, and she might have done mischief there. A person who don't mind hurting a girl's feelings, any more than she does, wouldn't mind hurting a robin's feelings."

As Jane drew near the place where the nest was, she did not see the little fan that attracted her attention the day before. She stole carefully up to the fence, and peeped over the rail, and saw three little birds in the nest, with their feathers well grown, and

their eyes wide open, and " winking away,"
as she said.

She imitated the sound of a kiss, and
they all opened their mouths, and she
wished she had something to feed them.
She was just about to look for some berries,
when *peep, peep,* said an old robin, flying
near her head ; *peep, peep,* said another robin,
coming from a neighboring tree.

"That's the papa, and that's the mamma, I suppose," said Jane. "You need not
think I am going to hurt your babies, only
please let me smooth them ; " and she put
out her hand towards the nest, but the old
birds set up such a cry, that she drew it
back, and retired, and stood at some distance
from the nest. One of the old birds then
flew to it, and then flew away again.

" There," said Jane, just as though the
robin could understand her, " you see I
have not hurt them. I wish you would not
be so foolish." But she soon thought she
was the foolish one for saying so. The
birds acted as they were made to act.

Jane went up and took another look at
the birds before she bade them good-by.

"What good-tempered things they must be," said she, as she stood looking at them, "to lie so close together in this hot weather, and not quarrel! I wonder if they always mind their mamma. Chickens always do; and birds are prettier than chickens; and so they must always mind."

According to Jane's logic, the best-looking children would always be the most obedient to their parents. But I have not always found that to be the case.

When Jane got home, she said, "Mother, why don't you, when you pray, why don't you thank the Lord for the birds?"

"They thank him themselves, in their songs, I presume."

"You don't understand me. Why don't you thank the Lord for making birds?"

"I have taught you to bless him for all his works. But what are you thinking of now?"

"I was thinking that, as they make us so happy, we ought to thank the Lord for them, as well as for food and clothing."

"Certainly, we ought to."

Jane helped her mother in her work, as

much as she could, for it was her washing-day; "but her head," she said, "*was full of robins all day.*"

Would the reader like to hear a part of Jane's prayer that night?

"O Lord, I thank thee for making robins and other little birds. I thank thee for letting me find the nest, on the rail fence, and the dear little ones in it. I pray thee to take care of them, and make them grow up to sing thy praise. I thank thee for all the happiness I have had to-day. I pray thee to forgive every thing I have done wrong to-day. Keep me safe while I sleep, and make me a comfort to mother. Our Father, who art in heaven" — ending with the Lord's prayer.

Is there any one disposed to despise such a simple prayer? The great God never despises a simple, heartfelt prayer. He loves to have his creatures come to him with all their joys and sorrows, and he is never weary of listening to what is said in a childlike spirit.

CHAPTER IX.

EMILY'S VISIT TO JANE.

One Saturday afternoon Jane had a visit from a little girl who lived nearly two miles distant. Her father, who had been a near neighbor of Jane's mother when they were both young, came to attend to some business in the village, and brought his daughter to spend the afternoon with the daughter of his friend.

Emily was about Jane's age. She was a beautiful little girl. If you had seen them together, you would have said she was handsomer than Jane, but that there was something about Jane's looks that made you like her best.

The girls soon got acquainted, and passed the afternoon very pleasantly. Towards night, they prepared to play tea in Jane's playhouse under the apple-tree. Mrs. L. offered to furnish them with bread and butter, but they chose to furnish all things themselves. So they gathered some strawberries, which were very ripe and good, and some currants and apples, which were green, and only for show. They had leaves for plates, and clam-shells for fruit dishes. Whatever the reader may think of it, they enjoyed it very much.

When it drew towards evening, Jane said she must put up all her things, for the morrow was the Sabbath.

"O, I wish there wasn't any Sundays," said Emily.

"Why, Emily, what do you mean by saying so?"

"Why, it is so dull. Mamma won't let me play; and there is nothing going on. It seems as if it never would be night. Don't you think Sundays are a great deal longer than other days?"

"No. They seem to me to be shorter; they pass away too soon."

"Why, now! what do you do? Do you always go to meeting?"

"Yes. Don't you?"

No. Sometimes we don't get breakfast

time enough to get ready; and sometimes papa guesses it is going to rain; and sometimes the wagon is broken; and sometimes papa is too tired;—so we don't go very often."

"Why, I never heard of such a thing!"

"Don't your mother ever stay home from meeting?"

"No, indeed."

"Don't she ever get tired?"

"I guess she does, but she says it always rests her to go to meeting."

"Well, I declare, she is different from my mother."

This remark was a very true one. Jane felt thankful that it was so: "For," thought she, "if she hadn't been, I should have been as much of a heathen as she is, poor girl!"

Now, Emily was not poor, so far as property was concerned, for her father was the owner of a large and fertile farm. But how much better is it to be poor, and yet be taught the fear of God, than to be rich, and be left to grow up in ignorance and sin!

5

" What do you do when meeting is out ?'
said Emily.

"I read the Bible, and talk with mother."

" What do you talk about ? "

" We talk about good things."

" We always have good things for supper,
Sunday nights."

"I don't mean good things to eat. We
talk about God and heaven."

" We don't talk about such things at our
house. Do you love to talk about such
things ? "

"O, yes, dearly. Mother is always so
happy then."

" Don't you ever play a bit on Sunday ? "

" Why, no, indeed. Do you ever play on
the Sabbath ? "

"Mother says I mustn't; but she never
does any thing if I play a little."

Jane began to wish Emily would go
home. "I had no idea," thought she,
"that she was such a wicked girl; but
then she has had no one to teach her. I
should have been just like her, or worse, if
it had not been for mother, — and I did not
choose my mother; God gave her to me."

"I wish," said she to Emily, "you wouldn't play any to-morrow."

"What shall I do? Father will say he is too tired to go to meeting, for he has been hoeing corn all the week till to-day, and we shall all stay at home; and the day is *so* long."

"I'll tell you what to do. You ask your mother to talk to you about heaven."

"That wouldn't be interesting."

"Yes, it will, very. You see if it is not."

Jane was honest in making this remark. She had no idea but that Emily's mother could talk as well on divine things as her mother could.

"I don't believe that my mother knows much about heaven. I never heard her say any thing about it. But I'll ask her to-morrow."

When Emily had gone home, Jane felt very sorry for her. When she had put up all her things, she told her mother all that Emily had said, and by the time she had told it, she had talked herself into tears.

"Mother, when you pray to-night, I

want you to pray for her, and for her mother, and for all of them. Don't you think
she is to be pitied, mother ? "

" She is greatly to be pitied. She seems
to be a well-disposed girl, and would prob-
ably attend to instruction if she had any
one to teach her."

" Yes, I know she would, for she don't
make as if she knew every thing, as Hannah does."

Hannah was one of those persons who,
if you tell them any thing, says, " I know
it ; " or if you show them something new,
have always *seen it or something better
before.* Does the reader belong to this
class ?

Jane went to sleep that night, blessing
God that she was born of a pious mother.

CHAPTER X.

THE SABBATH — CHURCH — SABBATH SCHOOL.

THE next morning, which was the Sabbath, Mrs. L. and her daughter rose as early as usual, that is, before the stars had quite faded from the sky.

"This is the day the Lord hath made; we will rejoice in it and be glad!" said Mrs. L.

"I am always glad when Sabbath comes," said Jane.

"Why?"

"Because you don't have to work, and we can go to meeting and hear Mr. M. preach, and to the Sabbath school, and I can sit and talk with you without your pricking your fingers by minding what I say; and it is not so easy to forget to pray and do right on Sabbath, as it is on week days. And besides, it almost always seems

5 *

as though the sky was brighter, and the birds sang more, than on other days. I don't know as it is so, but it seems so."

Mrs. L. was pleased with most of the reasons which Jane gave for loving the Sabbath. She did not know but that all of them were proper ones: indeed, she was sure they were, provided other and more important things held the first place.

"The great reason you have not mentioned," said Mrs. L.

"What is that?"

"The means the Sabbath furnishes for receiving instruction and gaining strength to get to heaven."

"I meant that in what I said about going to meeting, and Sabbath school, and talking with you; for we always talk about such things, you know."

This conversation took place while they were dressing. They never left their room on Sabbath morning without kneeling beside the bed and offering a prayer.

They next prepared their breakfast. Jane set the table, while her mother made a fire and put on the teakettle. Breakfast was soon ready, and they sat down, and Jane asked a blessing.

"It don't take us long to get breakfast, does it, mother?"

"Not long."

"I don't see how some folks can be so long about it. Emily says, sometimes they don't get breakfast out of the way in time to get ready for church."

"I presume they don't rise as early as on other mornings."

"Don't rise as early on the Sabbath as on days when they have work to do?"

Jane evidently did not know the habits of many families, where religion is professed: otherwise she would not have regarded late rising as so decided a mark of heathenism. If she had known more about the habits of such families, her ideas perhaps would have been different; but would they have been more correct?

When breakfast was over, they had prayers, and the things were cleared away and the floor swept, and they were ready to sit down to reading the Scriptures. Mrs. L. sat in her rocking-chair, and Jane placed her little chair by her side. Both had Bibles in their hands. Mrs. L. bent forward, and, putting the hair back from her forehead, kissed Jane before they began to read. They usually read for about an hour in silence. Jane had a lead pencil, and marked such verses as she could not understand, for her mother to explain to her.

Does any one ask why Jane didn't take this time to get her Sabbath school lesson? She had learned it the first part of the week before. It never seemed to her that it was right for her to put it off until Sabbath morning.

When Mrs. L. shut up her book, Jane asked her about the meaning of the passages she had marked. They spent their time in conversing in this manner until it was time to get ready for church.

It did not take them long to dress. They never spent any time in considering what dress they should wear. Each had one that was decent, and it was worn on every Sabbath. Before Mr. Ferry sent Jane the new calico I told you about, Jane once said to her mother, "I am most ashamed to wear this frock, I have worn it so long;" but she saw that the remark gave her mother pain, and she resolved she would never say any thing of that kind again, whatever she might think or feel. And on further reflection, she concluded there must have been something in the remark wrong in itself; "for my mother never feels bad about any thing I do, unless it is wrong."

Then they walked to the church, which was about three quarters of a mile distant. They were never absent, even when the weather was so bad that those who lived opposite the church could not come.

The manner in which Jane entered the church, and walked up the aisle, and conducted herself during the services, showed very clearly that to her they were far from being a weariness. She always came in with such a bright face and smile, that people loved to look at her. During prayers, she always bowed her head, and kept perfectly still. She found the hymns in her own little hymn-book; and if she knew the tune, she joined in singing. During sermon, she kept her eye fixed on the minister. She could not understand all that he said, but she understood a good deal, and oftentimes he addressed something especially to children ; and then he was so much engaged in what he said, and *looked so good*, as Jane said, that it was pleasant to listen to him even when the truth was beyond her comprehension. And she said once very sensibly, "Mother, if I don't try to understand what grown folks do, I never shall understand it."

I will repeat another of her remarks relating to this subject : "Mother, don't you think I understand more of the hard part of the sermon, than the grown folks do who sleep all the time ?"

The Sabbath school was held after the morning service. Mrs. L. was a teacher in it. Some thought that she worked hard enough during the week to excuse her from this labor. But she did not think so, and it was to her a labor of love.

Her class was always full, and they always had their lessons ; and yet they never seemed to have finished their recitation when it came time to dismiss the school

Some teachers hurry through with the lesson, lest the class should get tired; but somehow Mrs. L.'s class never seemed to get tired.

Jane would like to have been in her mother's class, but it consisted of large girls.

For some time, Jane's class had for their teacher a young lady who was said to be well educated and highly accomplished. She dressed very handsomely, and was always very polite to the members of the class. She was very regular in her attendance, and always asked all the questions in the lesson, and explained the difficult ones very well. But Jane thought she didn't seem to care much about what she taught. If Jane felt especially interested in the lesson, she didn't notice it. If a child asked a question which she thought was silly, she let her opinion of it appear by her manner, and very soon they all ceased to ask questions, for fear she would think they were silly.

If the reader must know, she was one of those who think they are highly intellectual, and that such a character is inconsistent with sympathy with the thoughts and feelings of a child.

There was a teacher of a class of boys who had their seats near by, who used to get so engaged in talking to his class that he would forget himself, and speak so loud as to be heard by the classes in the vicinity. You never saw a vacant seat in the pew where his class sat. One of the boys described him to a friend in these words: " He seems just like a boy that knows every thing, and the bell always rings before we think of it." He meant the bell for closing the school.

Jane's teacher thought he might be a very good man, but that he could not be very intellectual, and talk so much like a child. But it turned out that people in general differed from her in their opinion of him, for, while he was yet young, he was chosen governor of the state.

When this intellectual teacher thought she had discharged her duty, she retired from the school, and a plain-looking girl, dressed in a cheap calico, took her place.

Jane thought she acted as though she thought she could not teach ; but she could smile, and very sweetly too, and that Jane thought was an important qualification for a Sabbath school teacher, and older persons have thought so too. After school was out, the superintendent asked Jane how she liked her new teacher.

"Very much," said Jane. "I think she will be as interesting as mother, when she gets to be as old."

After meeting was out in the afternoon, Mrs. L. and Jane came home, and got their tea, for they went without dinner. They then usually sat down, and spent a long time in conversation. I will give you a specimen of their conversation, at such times, in the next chapter.

CHAPTER XI.

CONVERSATION ABOUT ANGELS.

AFTER tea, which they had as soon as they returned from church in the afternoon, Mrs. L. and her daughter were accustomed to spend a long time in conversation. They always began with the sermons they had heard. They did not criticise and find fault with them. The object was to fix the most important truths they contained firmly in the memory. They then passed on to such other subjects as promised to be interesting and useful.

On the Sabbath of which I am now speaking, a stranger preached. The discourse of the preacher related to the nature and ministry of angels, but it had not the simplicity which was necessary to render any considerable portion of it intelligible to a child.

Jane was much interested in the subject,

and was very anxious to get the tea things out of the way, that her mother might talk to her about it.

"Mother, the minister said that angels were invisible spirits, and their presence could not be known by our senses. Didn't they use to be visible? I read, this morning, about the angel who let Peter out of prison. Did not Peter see him?"

"Yes, Peter, no doubt, saw him. They have power given them, on special occasions, to assume a visible appearance."

"Did they look just like men then?"

"It is probable that they bore an exact resemblance to the human form, for the angels who brought Lot out of Sodom were mistaken for men by the people of that city."

'What do the angels have to do?"

"They have God's will to do."

"I know that, but they don't have the same kind of work to do for the Lord that we do."

"A part of their employment is to take care of those whom the Lord loves. Turn to Hebrews, first chapter and seventh verse, and read."

"Are they not all ministering spirits, sent forth to minister for them who shall be heirs of salvation?"

"Do the angels love us, mother?"

"I presume they do, for the Lord's sake. What passage of Scripture can you think of which shows that they feel a deep interest in the welfare of men?"

Jane thought for a moment, and then repeated, "'There is joy in heaven, among the angels of God, over one sinner that repenteth.' Mother, are the angels often near us?"

"It is probable they are. It is reasonable to suppose that they are often near to those whom they serve."

"May be there are angels in the room with us now."

"It is quite possible, my dear."

"If I really thought there were any here, I should be afraid," said Jane, drawing her chair close to her mother.

"If there are any here, they are only to do us good. They are pure and holy fellow-servants of the same Master."

" If they are always with us, must it not make them feel bad when we do wrong? "

" It certainly must grieve them to see God dishonored, especially by those who have been redeemed by the blood of his Son."

" Is not this another reason why we should be careful not to sin, especially in secret? If every body remembered that the angels were looking at them, it would restrain them as much as if men were looking at them. And you know we are often ashamed to do wrong before folks."

" I am afraid not: all men know that God is always looking at them, but it does not restrain them from secret sins."

" That is true, mother. Do good people when they die, become angels? "

" No : they become perfect spirits."

" I heard Miss R. read a piece of poetry about a little babe that died, and I remember this line —

' Thou art an angel now.' "

" After death, the pious become ' like to the angels.' But, properly speaking, the angels are another order of beings."

6 *

"Can the spirits of the pious dead come about us as the angels can?"

"I do not know."

"O, I wish they could: then papa's spirit would be always with us."

"It may be so; but we are not certainly informed about it."

"I think that is another reason why we should be careful not to sin. How I should hate to have my father see his little daughter doing wrong!"

This allusion to her departed husband disposed Mrs. L. to meditation rather than conversation, and she told Jane she would take up the subject again at another time.

CHAPTER XII.

MR. AND MRS. THORNE — TEA WITHOUT TEA
— ANOTHER VISIT TO THE ROBIN'S NEST.

MR. AND MRS. THORNE were seated at their breakfast-table, and as many of their children as had risen were with them. The room was large and richly furnished. The table was spread with a great variety of food.

Mr. Thorne was very neatly dressed, and seemed prepared to go out. Mrs. T. had on a loose dress, and something that looked like a nightcap, underneath which peeped out certain bunches of paper.

"Mr. Thorne, if you have a quarter in your pocket, I beg you will leave it with me, to pay that woman with. She pesters my life out of me, by calling for it."

"To pay whom?" said Mr. Thorne, feeling in his ample pockets for the money.

"Mrs. L.: I can't be annoyed so; my nerves won't bear it."

Mr. Thorne found a piece which he supposed to be a quarter, and handed it to her; but just as it was passing out of his hand, he saw it was a gold piece. "Hold on; that is an eagle!"—and after a time he succeeded in finding the sum in question, and handed it to her, saying, in a soothing tone, "The poor are always querulous: you must not mind it."

The annoyance to which Mrs. Thorne was subject may be learned from the following incidents. Mrs. L. had done a small piece of sewing for Mrs. Thorne, and sent it home by Jane. Mrs. T. said nothing about paying for it. After a long time, Mrs. L. sent Jane to ask for it, and she was told she must call again. After some weeks' further delay, Mrs. L., being in want of some tea, called herself, and was told that Mrs. T. was engaged. This was on the evening before the occurrence of the conversation which I have related as having taken place between Mr. and Mrs. Thorne. The reader will judge how great the annoyance to which Mrs. T. was subjected.

Mrs. L. was obliged to do without tea that morning. But that Jane might not feel unhappy, she boiled some water as usual, and poured it into the teapot, and poured out into her cup, and drank it. Jane did not know there was no tea in the teapot. I have told you that she always drank cold water.

"Is it right," thought Mrs. L., "thus to deceive my child?" She was not sure that it was. She in consequence resolved that she would not do it again. Her rule was, never to do a thing if she were not sure it was right. It was a rule which she very carefully taught her daughter. It is a rule that every one should learn to practise.

Soon after breakfast, a boy came from Mrs. Thorne and brought the money. Mrs. L. purchased some tea, and was thus saved from the temptation of deceiving her daughter again.

As soon as Jane had done up her work, she went to visit her robin's nest. She found that the young robins had grown very much since she had last seen them. They now filled the nest more than full.

She put out her hand to smooth them, and one of them hopped out of the nest, and flew to a short distance. Jane ran and caught him, and put him back in the nest, and then the two others flew out. She caught one, but the other flew so far that she lost sight of him. She held the one she had caught for some time, in hopes that he would get over his fright; but as soon as she put him in the nest, he flew away, and was followed by the remaining one, so that the nest was now empty.

Jane was now in great trouble. She was afraid that they would get lost and die, and that she should be the cause of their death. She came home weeping, and told her mother all her troubles.

"The old birds will take care of them, my dear."

"Will they make them go back to the nest?" .

"They will make them go back if they wish to have them. If not, they will take care of them. They make them leave their nest as soon as they are able to fly a little, that they may use their wings. If you had not scared them out, the old ones would have made them go out very soon. Perhaps you have saved them some trouble."

"Why do they wish to have them leave the nest before they can fly away off?"

"They never would be able to fly, in that case. If the old birds were to do so, they would be as foolish as the man who resolved that he would never go into the water till he had learned to swim. The young ones have to learn to fly, just as you had to learn to walk. They gain strength and skill by every trial : very soon they will be able to fly as well as the old birds."

"But what if something should catch them before they are able to fly so?"

"You would be sorry, but I don't see as you can help it."

"I wish robins had been made so that they could defend themselves."

"I suppose you could make them better than the Lord has seen fit to."

"No, ma'am, I didn't mean that — only — I didn't think. I suppose I need not feel uneasy, for the Lord will take care of them better than I could."

" My daughter, say so in your heart in regard to all things. When you have done your duty, leave the event with God, and be content."

Jane sat down to assist her mother in some plain sewing, and they kept silence for a long time. At length Jane broke silence. "Mother, I have been thinking, that I don't trust the Lord only when I can't help it ; and that is not right."

" I don't apprehend your meaning."

" Well, if I didn't mind you only when I couldn't help it, what would you think of me ? "

" I don't know what idea you have in your head," said her mother, smiling.

" Well, when I am anxious and troubled about any thing, as I was about the birds, I worry myself, and try to do something, till I find I can't, and then I cast my care on the Lord. I ought to cast my care on the Lord first, and then do all I can. Is not that the way ? "

" It is certainly the way we ought to do. I am glad to see you get clear ideas of duty.

But to know our duty is one thing ; to per-
form it is another."

"I know that, mother."

" Remember, the more you know of duty,
the greater your obligation to do it, and the
greater your need of the grace of God."

7

CHAPTER XIII.

THE DESERTED NEST — THE ROBIN IN THE CAGE — ENVY.

JANE visited the nest the next day at an early hour, and found it deserted. She had a faint hope that the old birds had made them go back to it; but there were no birds there. She could not help crying when she thought that she should never see them again.

She was returning home when a neighbor's boy, a few years older than she was, met her, and asked her what she was crying about. "Have you lost all your relations?"

"No; but my birds have flown away, and I can't find them."

"What birds were they?"

"Little robins."

"Where did you keep them?"

"There, in the nest on the rail fence."

"O, you goose you! I thought you had them in a cage, and that they had got out."

He was passing on, when he stopped and said, " Here, you! I'll give you a robin if you'll come to our house after it."

"I shouldn't like to rob the old bird of its young ones."

" There won't be much robbery about it. I killed the old one. It is in a cage; but I shall get tired of feeding it, and you may have it, if you want it." And he went on whistling in a way which he called whistling at a mark. •

Jane told him she would ask her mother about it; but he did not stop to hear what she said.

She went to her mother about as quickly as her little feet could carry her. "Mother, I want to tell you something. Thomas Green says he has a robin in a cage, that he will give to me; and he has killed the old bird, and he is tired of feeding it, and I may have it if I will come after it: may I go, mother?"

" It will be a great deal of trouble to take care of it."

" But, mother, you know, care is not trouble when we love any thing."

Mrs. L. was delighted that her daughter had learned a truth so necessary to the endurance and enjoyment of life. She granted the desired permission, and soon Jane was on her way home with her prize. The cage was loaned her for a time.

She noticed, as she went along with the cage in her hand, that a robin followed her at some distance, and now and then would fly over her head quite near her. "I wonder," said she to herself, "if that is not one of the old birds. He didn't say that he killed both of them."

She set the cage down under a tree beside the road, and retired a little way from it, to see if the old bird wouldn't go up to it; and sure enough, it went to the cage, and the little one came and put his head through the wires, and opened his mouth to be fed.

"Now, old birdie," said Jane, as she took up the cage, "you go home with me, and you shall have a nice place to feed your baby in; and when he gets big, you shall have him to fly away with you, unless I can persuade him to stay with me, and live with folks."

The old bird followed her home. She put the cage in her playhouse, under the tree, and ran to her mother.

"Mother, I've got my bird, and his mamma has come with him: do come and see!"

Mrs. L. laid aside her sewing, and followed her daughter. "See, mother; do see; she is feeding him already!"

The old bird had found a worm, and was dropping it in the young one's mouth.

"Now, mother, I will watch and see what she gives him, and will help her feed him."

"I don't think she will be exhausted by the care of one bird."

"But, mother, she has got to do it all alone, for the other old bird is dead."

"So you will take his place?"

"Yes, mother;" and the idea pleased her very much. She went up to the cage, and said, "Birdie, I'm the other old birdie;" and the little robin said *peep*, and opened his mouth to be fed.

"I declare," said Jane, "he owns me already!"

The old bird now made her appearance

7 *

again.   She had a strawberry in her mouth,
which she gave to the young one.

"Mother, she is giving him strawberries,"
said Jane, in so loud a voice that her mother
was led to say, "Don't scream so; you will
make him think you are a hawk instead of
the old bird.   I never heard a robin make
such a noise."

"Well, I'm so happy, I forgot; please
excuse me!" and away she ran to get some
strawberries.   She soon returned with some
fine ripe ones.   She smacked her lips to the
little bird, and he opened his mouth, and
she dropped one in, and he swallowed it, to
her great delight.   He opened his mouth
again, but she didn't succeed so well this
time.   "I can't do it as well as the other
old bird, but I shall learn."

She kept on till he had eaten five, and
then he would not open his mouth any
more.   "I guess he has had enough — I'll
leave these here for the old bird; perhaps
she will want them."   So she laid them
beside the cage, and went in to her mother.

"Mother, do old birds ever feed one another?"

"I can't say. Perhaps they do."

"Well, I've put some strawberries on a leaf for the other old bird."

"I doubt whether she will appreciate your kind intentions."

Jane then went out to see her charge, but soon came running in. "Mother, he likes the other old bird the best; for he is taking a berry from her, and he wouldn't take one from me."

"I hope you don't feel envious toward your mate?"

"I don't know exactly what you mean by envious."

"I hope you never will, from experience. Persons are envious when they see others have more things than they have, or receive more attention than they do."

"If they came honestly by their things, what right has any person to say any thing about it, or feel bad? I think it is very foolish."

"It certainly is, and very wrong; but there is a great deal of it in the world."

"Is there any body envious of me?" said Jane, after keeping silence for some time.

"I don't know," said Mrs. L., smiling in rather a sad manner : "you have not many things that are often the subjects of envy. Envious persons look towards those who have more sources of enjoyment than they have themselves."

"Is Mr. Holland an envious man ?"

"What makes you ask such a question? I don't know his heart; but, from all I have seen of him, he is one of the last persons to be suspected of envy. What led you to ask that question ?"

"I remember, a great while ago, when we children were playing, he came along with another man, and said, 'I envy that child her light heart.' I knew he meant me, but didn't know what he meant by saying so."

"Mr. Holland did not use the term *envy* in its true sense; he meant to express his pleasure at seeing you so cheerful and happy."

"You said envious persons did not look at those who had fewer means of happiness. Are not we as happy as other folks ?"

"I have never been in the habit of

making comparisons. We are a great deal happier than we deserve to be."

" Well, mother, I have often thought — I know you have to work hard, and when I get older I can help you more, so that you won't have to sit up so late — I have often thought that we are happier than almost any body else. When I go to —— " She hesitated naming the family, and her mother supplied the words "some places."

" Yes, ma'am : when I go to some places, they often speak short and cross to one another, and it makes me feel very uncomfortable; and when they talk pleasantly, it seems as if they didn't mean it. I don't believe they are as happy as we are, with all their carpets and fine things. It always looks cold and gloomy there. It always looks pleasant here, even when it rains."

" A contented mind is a perpetual feast."

" Where do we get contented minds ? Don't God give them to us ? "

" Yes, my dear, if we have them."

" Then we ought to be as thankful for them as for a feast."

" Certainly."

"Mr. Jones was wrong, then."

"In what?"

."Why, once when I was there, he was rebuking Abby for complaining of something; and I heard him say — he did not know that I heard him, and I didn't listen, neither, but I couldn't help hearing him — I heard him say, 'Look at little Jane; she don't complain: she hasn't as many things to be thankful for as you have.' Now, I think I have more things to be thankful for than she has; for I have a contented mind, besides a great many other things."

CHAPTER XIV.

SUSAN MILLAR — CONFESSION — JANE'S EXAMPLE.

LITTLE Susan Millar had left her playthings out over night, and they were, in consequence, injured by a fall of rain. When her father went along by her playhouse, he heard her crying at a great rate, and supposed she had hurt herself very badly. He inquired, and was sorry to learn that she had been crying for a long time over the trifling injury her toys had suffered from the rain.

"My daughter, don't be making such an outcry for so small a matter."

"It may be a small matter to you, but it ain't to me," said she. Now this was a very improper mode of speaking to a parent.

But her father was not sure that she meant any thing wrong, though the manner was very unpleasant to him. He did not reprove her for it then, but deferred it till another time.

"You should take things easily, as your friend Jane does. What do you suppose she would do, if the same accident should happen to her things?"

"She hasn't any things!" in about the same tone as before.

"I guess she has some, though she may not have as many as you have; but what she has are of as much consequence to her as yours are to you. What do you suppose she would do if she were in your place?"

"I don't know."

He saw that she was out of temper, and told her to go to her room and stay till her temper was in better order. He did not speak harshly, but in a manner which showed his disapprobation of her conduct.

Susan went to her chamber. Her conscience there told her that she had not honored her father, and that she had not spoken the truth when she said, "I don't know." She had no doubt but that Jane would have said something like this: "Well, the good Lord made it rain; I should not have left

them out ;" and would have made no com-
plaint, and would have got over feeling bad
in a very few moments.

Susan tried to excuse herself by saying
that she did not know for certain what
Jane would do in her circumstances ;
but that did not satisfy her conscience.
The meaning of her father's question was,
what *she supposed* Jane would do — what
she thought Jane would do.

Conscience told her that, if she had spoken
the truth, she would have said, " I suppose
she would have found out some reason for
not minding it, as she always does when she
has any trouble."

Susan saw that this was the true answer.
She was sorry she had not given it. She
was honest enough to confess to herself that
she had told an untruth. This was the first
step towards reformation.

She knew that the next step would be to
go and confess her fault to her father. But
she felt ashamed to. When she remembered how carefully her father had impressed
this rule on her mind, " Never be ashamed
to do right," she resolved she would go

to him and confess. So she came to her
father, with a very downcast look and red
face, and said, " Father, I am sorry I spoke
so naughtily to you ; and I did not speak
the truth when I said I didn't know what
Jane would do, and ———— " Her tears pre-
vented her saying any thing more, and she
hid her face in her father's bosom.

" My dear daughter," — kissing her ten-
derly, while a tear fell from his eye upon her
cheek, — " I forgive you, and so will God, if
you ask him."

She soon dried her tears, and her father
took her on his knee, and they conversed
very pleasantly. She had read in her school
book — " Blessings on the man that invented
sleep ! " and she said to herself, " Blessings
on the man that invented confession ! "

Her father now repeated the question respecting Jane, and she answered it truly.

" Why is it, daughter, that Jane always
takes things so easily and pleasantly ? "

"It is because she has such a cheerful
disposition."

" What is there to hinder you from having such a cheerful disposition ? "

" We don't make our own dispositions — they are given us."

" Well, if we don't make our natural dispositions, we can improve them by cultivation. I have known a piece of land which was very poor, made, by culture, the richest piece I ever saw. So, a disposition that is not amiable by nature may be made lovely by cultivation."

" Well, I'm sure I should like to be as cheerful and good as Jane, if I could."

" You certainly can, my dear."

" How, papa ? "

" By doing as she does — that is, when she does right : no person is to be imitated in all things, for no one is perfect."

" She is not always with me, so that I can see what she does."

" You can think how it is probable she would act, in a given case ; and if your reason and conscience approve it, you can act so too."

" Well, father, I will try to imitate her good qualities."

I hope the reader will do so too.

CHAPTER XV.

JOINING THE CHURCH.

One Sabbath morning, after breakfast, Mrs. L. and her daughter were reading in their Bibles according to their usual custom. Jane's attention did not seem so well fixed on what she read as usual. She often looked off from her book, and seemed buried in thought, and often looked up to her mother, as if she wished to ask her something. Her mother at length noticed it, and, closing her book sooner than usual, awaited her daughter's questions.

"Mother, what does this passage mean — 'Whosoever, therefore, shall confess me before men, him will I confess also before my Father which is in heaven'? What is meant by 'confess me before men'?"

"To acknowledge him as the Saviour, and to serve him openly."

"I didn't know but that it meant something else."

"What else, my dear?"

"I didn't know but that it meant that all who are Christians — that is, all who think they are Christians — should confess him before men by joining the church."

"It is doubtless the duty of all such to unite with the church at the proper time, — though this passage was not intended to teach that particular duty."

"What is the proper time, mother?"

"When there is satisfactory evidence that the person is truly a Christian. Some time is necessary to show this."

"How old must persons be before they can have this evidence?"

"I cannot say."

Mrs. L. now understood what was passing in her daughter's mind. She saw that, under the teachings of the Word and the Spirit of God, she was coming to a point to which she had long desired her to come, viz., a public profession of religion. She had long been satisfied that her daughter was numbered

8 *

among God's chosen ones; but, owing to l er tender age, she had never thought it wise to propose to her to become a member of the visible church.

"My daughter, tell me your thoughts and wishes on this subject without reserve."

"I was thinking — that it might be my duty — if I was not too young — to join the church."

"Do you wish to do so?"

"Yes, ma'am, and I have wished to for a long time."

"Why do you desire to do so?"

"I suppose the Lord wants all who love him to belong to his church; and always on communion days I feel as though I wanted to obey Christ when he says, "*Do this in remembrance of me;*" and then, if I belonged to the church, I should have a share in the prayers that are always offered for it."

Mrs. L. was too much overcome to carry on the conversation. She retained her composure sufficiently long to tell her daughter that she would ask the minister to talk with her on the subject. She then retired to her closet, and relieved herself by shedding delicious tears as she offered her thanksgivings to God.

Jane was a little troubled by her mother's departure : she was afraid she had said what her mother did not approve. But when she came out of her closet with such a beaming countenance, all her anxiety was removed.

In a few days, Mr. M., the minister, called, at Mrs. L.'s request, and had a long conversation with Jane, respecting her views and feelings on the subject of religion. I shall relate only a part of the conversation.

"Why do you think you are a Christian, Jane ? "

" There are a good many reasons why I hope I am a Christian. I love Christ; I love to do his will; I love his people; I love to pray — sometimes, almost always."

" You love Christ because he has done so much for you ? "

" I suppose that is a good reason, but I never thought much about reasons. It seems to me that if any one only sees

Christ, he can't help loving him. I love him because I can't help it."

"Did you always love him?"

"No, sir. I can remember that when mother used to talk to me, it used to seem as if there wasn't any such person. I don't mean that I did not believe all she said, but it didn't seem real. I used to pray then, but it didn't seem as if I was praying to any thing. But once, when I felt very bad because I was so wicked, it seemed to come all at once to me that there was a Christ, and all that I had read and heard about him seemed real; and then I couldn't help loving him."

"Could you pray any better after that?"

"Yes, sir; it always seemed as if he heard me after that."

"Has it always been easy to pray since then?"

"Not always. Sometimes, when I have been so busy that I have forgotten to pray when the time came, and sometimes when I have been naughty, and have not repented, it has seemed hard work to pray."

"Are you ever naughty?"

"Yes, sir, sometimes, and a great deal more so than any body knows."

"How is that?"

"I have a great many wicked thoughts, that no one but God can see."

"Do they give you any trouble, if no one knows them?"

"Yes, sir; God knows them — and I sometimes fear that I am not a Christian; for if I was, it seems to me I should not have so many wicked thoughts in my mind."

"Do you love to have them?"

"O, no, sir. I try to keep them out of my mind."

"Do you think, on the whole, that you are good enough to belong to the church — good enough for God to love you?"

"I don't think I'm good enough for any thing. I hope that God loves me for Christ's sake."

Mr. M. reported the case to the church at the next meeting, and it was voted that she be received as a member.

The Sabbath on which she was to make

a public profession of her faith came. The report that a child was to be publicly received into the church caused the edifice to be crowded to the full.

The morning discourse was ended, and the candidate was requested to present herself. Jane left her seat, and walked with a timid step up the broad aisle to the open space in front of the desk. She was alone. There was none other in that large assembly ready to confess the Saviour before men. Her face was pale, and the smile with which she usually entered the house of God was wanting. But what a depth of meaning in that full dark eye!

There was the silence of death as she sweetly and solemnly responded to the questions that were proposed to her, and took the vows of God upon her; and many a head was bowed, and many a cheek was moistened.

The senior deacon, who, for forty years past, had always, on such occasions, stood upright at the foot of the pulpit, facing the congregation, and whose self-control was such that a slight moistening of the eye was all the external showing of emotion ever visible, was obliged to sit down, bury his face in his hands, and sob aloud.

A hoary-headed sinner who was present exclaimed, when the services had closed, "I have stood out against preaching and praying all my life, but I can't stand that. I'm determined to seek for salvation."

Where was the mother? There are *joys with which a stranger intermeddleth not.*

CHEERFUL OBEDIENCE.

"PAPA," said Caroline, "I don't know as I fully understood what you said about the different kinds of obedience."

"I will illustrate them by a story."

"Pray do," said Caroline, folding her arms, and preparing to give her eager attention.

"I have no doubt you will give good attention to the story part; but whether the point to be illustrated will be attended to or not, I don't know."

"Why, papa," said Caroline, a little hurt, "I always attend to that. I love to hear the story, but I always wish to know what it means."

"Well, daughter, I will proceed. Mr. Anson told his son James, who was a little boy, that he wished him to take a letter to the post-office for him. 'O dear,' said James, almost crying, 'I was just going to play.' Still he began immediately to prepare to go, according to his father's request, and he very soon came and asked for the letter."

"Well, papa," said Caroline, "is not that as it should be ? He immediately proceeded to do what his father wished him to do. Was not that obeying him ?"

"Yes, daughter, it was very well so far as immediate obedience was concerned ; but there was a want of cheerful obedience. The expression of reluctance was wrong. It looked as though he obeyed only from compulsion ; and obedience from compulsion, or even fear, can hardly be called obedience."

"I don't see why."

"Suppose I tell you to go into the garden and pluck one of your moss-roses for me : you are unwilling to do so ; you have no wish to oblige me. Well, now suppose there is an invisible hand which forcibly leads you into the garden, and causes you to pluck the rose and bring it to me. You do what I told you to do; but could that properly be called obedience?"

"Certainly not; and I see that if James went to the post-office only because he knew he would be obliged to, his going could not properly be called obedience. Still it was not so bad as if he had said he would not go — was it?"

"By no means. And further, I do not suppose that James prepared to go because he knew or thought he would be obliged to go. He was accustomed to obey; but he often failed to render cheerful obedience."

"Perhaps James was sorry for what he had said before he got ready to go. You know we, at least I, sometimes speak before I think, and am sorry as soon as the words are out of my mouth. I have sometimes felt sorry to leave off playing when mother wanted me to do something for her; but as soon as I had time to think, I wished to please her — I was sorry because I was sorry; maybe it was so with James."

"When he came for the letter, his face was bright, and his father hoped the case was as you have supposed. In order to test the state of James's mind, he told him he need not go. 'I wish to go, sir,' said James. 'Why do you wish to go?' said his father. Now, what do you think was the answer?"

"I don't know," said Caroline. "I guess it was, because he wished to oblige his father."

"It was no such thing. His reply was, 'I wish to see if my newspaper has come!' After all, there was a selfish motive at the bottom of his obedience, if obedience it could be called. He had no wish to oblige his father. His father told him he need not go at all if he could not go to oblige him. He then carried his letter to the post-office himself."

"Didn't James beg to go?"

"No; he went to his play just as if nothing had happened."

"Is it possible?"

"And what made the matter worse, the day before this happened, his father had laid aside his work for some time to make James a little ship, and he had to sit up very late that night to make up for lost time."

"I should not think his father would ever make any thing for him again."

"Parents, you know, do not ask how their children like to be treated, but in what way they can be made good and happy. I hope you will be very careful to avoid James's fault — indeed, I am sure you will. Obey cheerfully, and you will not only make your parents happy, but you will please God."

9 *

SUBMISSION.

LITTLE Julia expected to make a visit to a friend in the afternoon, if it did not rain. She was very desirous of making the visit, and of course was anxious about the weather. It began to cloud up. A few drops of rain fell, and then the sun shone out again. Julia went very often to the door to observe the appearance of the sky. The last time she went, it looked very dark and threatening. Julia could hardly keep from crying, as she thought of losing her visit. She did make out to keep the tears out of her eyes, and said, in a tone of submission, "I suppose it will be just as the good Lord sees fit."

"I don't believe," said James, "that the Lord has any thing to do with it. When it is a-going to rain, it rains, and when it isn't, it don't."

"Why, James! have you never read that He sendeth rain on the just and unjust? This is the Lord's world, and he does with it just as he sees fit."

"Well, I wish he would not see fit to make it rain this afternoon, for I want to go a-fishing."

"O James! where have you been to learn to talk so? It is wicked, very wicked, to speak of the Lord so;" and the little girl shed tears over the sin of her brother.

"Well, sissy, I didn't mean to say so. I won't say so again."

He did not, in fact, see the full force of the expression till after he made it; still, he knew while he was making it, and before he began to make it, that it was not quite right. But he had an idea that there was something *smart* and *manly* about what he was going to say. Boys often do and say what they know is wrong, under the mistaken idea that it is manly. But if General Washington were alive, would any one think it manly to insult him? Is it manly to insult God?

About noon it began to rain. Julia was

constrained to give up her visit, and James his fishing excursion. Julia shed a few tears, but soon dried them, and came and sat down by her mother, and asked permission to assist her in sewing. There was a smile on her lips, though you could see that it required an effort to keep it there ; but she deserved so much the more credit on that account.

James bore his disappointment very well indeed. He felt conscious of having done wrong by speaking as he did in the morning, and he thought he would atone for it by making no complaints. It was right for him to refrain from making complaints ; but he ought to have known that doing our duty at one time, did not atone for neglecting it at another time.

" You are greatly disappointed, my dear, in regard to your visit, but I am glad to see that you have made up your mind to bear it like a woman."

" If the good Lord thinks it best to have it rain, I ought not to be sorry."

Her mother was sorry she had not said, " I am glad you have made up your mind to bear it like a Christian."

At this moment Julia's father came in, and remarked that it was a fine rain, and that vegetation needed it very much. "I think it is likely," said he, "that there will be a thousand bushels of corn more in this township than there would have been without this rain. The corn has suffered very much from the drought."

Julia felt ashamed of the anxiety she had felt during the morning that it should not rain. "How selfish," thought she, "I should be, if I could always have my own way!" She found some consolation in the recollection that she had submitted to the will of God before she was told of the advantages of the rain.

"O mother, how glad I am that God's will is done instead of mine!" said she.

"What are you thinking about?"

"I was thinking that if I had my will it would not have rained, and then there would have been a thousand bushels less of corn, and some of the people must have lacked bread, just because I wished to go a-visiting."

Julia then arose and went to the door

that opened into the garden. She saw the flowers, that were just now drooping, holding up their heads, and every thing looked green and refreshed. Again she felt an emotion of joy that God's will was done instead of hers.

"Mother," said she, as she resumed her seat, "the flowers are very glad it rains, and the grass, and the birds, — I suppose, though I don't know ; — they have not any roofs to their nests."

"My wren is pretty safe," said James.

"Where is your wren ?" said his father.

"In my hat."

"Have you been taking a wren prisoner ?"

"No, sir. I hung my old hat up in the stoop, and a wren has filled it half full of sticks, and built his nest in it. He don't care whether it rains or not."

"I saw you out in the sun without a hat. I meant to speak to you about it."

"You will be tanned as black as a mulatto," said his mother.

"Well, I didn't want to go out bareheaded; I didn't feel comfortable at all; but what could I do? The little fellow had worked so hard, and gathered so many sticks, that I could not bear to throw them away ; so I thought, as he had got my hat, he must keep it till his young ones get' big enough to fly away."

" As the hat was about worn out, I think you may as well let him have it ; but you should have asked me to get a new one. Did you expect to go bareheaded all summer ? "

" I don't know, sir. I didn't think much about it."

" Boys must think. They should never do any thing, and then say, ' I didn't think any thing about it.' They must always think before they act."

" Papa, what do the birds do, that haven't any hats, when it rains ? " said Julia.

" They have water-proof coats, which they put on when they think it is going to rain."

" What do you mean, papa ? "

" They have a little receptacle of oil, with which they oil their feathers, so that they shed rain as well as a piece of oiled cloth."

"I saw the old hen oiling her feathers. I didn't know what she was doing. She thought it was going to rain, I suppose."

"Papa, do the birds love to have it rain?"

"I can't tell you: they love to have it stop, I should judge by their actions on such occasions; and," rising up and going to the window, "I think it is going to stop now; it looks light in the west."

Sure enough, there was a light streak on the edge of the horizon, and soon a piece of blue sky appeared, and ere long the clouds had all rolled away into the far south, and the sun shone in all his glory. It was not so late but that Julia made her visit, and felt that she enjoyed it much more from the lesson of submission that she had taken in the morning.

THE END.